THERE'S A SKUNK IN MY BUNK
Helping Children Learn Tolerance

by

Joseph T. McCann, Psy.D.

Illustrations by
Thomas Gerlach

One night after finishing my very last chore
And putting on the pajamas that I usually wore,
I went downstairs for some juice and a snack.
As I started to eat, I heard a terrible *CRACK!*

It came from the room that my brother and I share.
We are good friends; people say we're quite a pair.
I gave a quick look across the room at my father;
I decided to check myself and not be a bother.
I didn't know if I should climb up that first stair
To see what had happened – I wasn't sure if I'd dare.
Then my curiosity got the best of me,
So I walked up the stairs to go and see.

Down the hall, I crept softly to the door of my room.
I quietly tiptoed then I heard a big *BOOM!*
For a moment I thought I should just run away,
When something inside of me told me to stay.
So I inched the door open; then I peeked inside.
I saw my bedroom window was open wide.

He said, "I was cold and needed a safe place to rest.
My name is Sam and I don't mean to be a pest."
"Well, my name is Timmy and this is my bunk.
How did you get in here?" I asked Sam the skunk.
"I was shivering outside on this freezing night,
When your brightly lit house came into my sight.
I climbed to your window, opened it wide,
Slipped over the sill and wiggled inside."

I became angry as Sam the skunk told his tale of woe.
I was sure I already knew about skunks all I needed to know.
"You're a skunk!" I exclaimed. "And skunks really smell.
The thought of you in my bed doesn't make me feel very well."
And I continued to tell him all the reasons why he
Should get out of my house and just let me be.

Sam stood his ground saying, "May I have a word?
All these bad things about me you have apparently heard,
Are they things that you've learned by meeting creatures like me?
Or are they things people told you that you think ought to be?"
I said nothing to him, unsure what to think.
He said, "I don't smell bad now, do I? I don't stink!"

"You're right, there's no odor," I said with surprise.
"That's just what I mean," he said, looking into my eyes.
"Sometimes people just accept the things they are told
Instead of allowing the truth to unfold.
That famous strong scent for which I am known,
Protects me, so enemies will leave me alone.
I don't have big teeth or fight very well,
So I scare them away with a very bad smell."

Sam seemed quite brave and eager to speak.

But he was interrupted by a sudden, sharp squeak.

With a bit of a jump, we both turned in the direction

Of the sound that had suddenly grabbed our attention.

On the sill of the window, peering into my room,

Sat a very inquisitive, wide-eyed raccoon.

"Hello, Ralph, my good friend," Sam said with a grin.

Ralph Raccoon jumped from the window and stepped right in.

Ralph looked about and then caught Sam's eye.
"I was afraid I lost you, friend," he said with a sigh.
"But I see you have found a warm resting place
And a nice young boy, with a friendly face."
Suddenly, from above, there came another loud sound.
Startled, Sam and Ralph glanced quickly around.
"Oh my!" said Sam. "What on earth could that be?"
Alarmed, Ralph stood up quickly and said, "Let's go see!"

But there was no way I would follow that creature anywhere;
I had been told raccoons were sneaky with that black mask of hair.
Then my new friend, Sam, pulled me by the hand.
"Hooray, an adventure! Now, isn't this grand?"
With Sam in the lead and Ralph close behind,
We tiptoed from the room to see what we would find.

We all stayed very quiet and were trying to hear,
When a flurry of noise seemed to come from quite near.
I stopped, listened and shivered with fright.
Oh, where was my courage on this scary night?
My new friends pushed and cheered me ahead,
Right up the stairs, far away from my bed.

We scurried upstairs and peeked into the room.
But now there was no noise, not a squeak or a boom.
Ralph walked in bravely and called out, "Who's there?"
We followed him closely. Could it be a big bear?
When, off in the corner, I noticed a spark,
A glimmer of light in the attic so dark.
Shaking, I moved closer and what did I see?
An upside down bat, staring straight at me.

"A bat!" I squealed loudly and covered my head.

Oh, how I wished that I were safe in my bed!

I cried out, "Please don't bite me or fly in my hair!"

But when I looked up again the bat wasn't there.

Suddenly, he landed on a box at my feet.

"Now why would I do that? You're too big to eat!"

Said the bat with a chuckle and a wink of his eye,

As Ralph and Sam watched from their seats close by.

I dropped my arms but still trembled with fear.

I asked, "Mr. Bat, what are you doing up here?"

"My name is Bob," he said with a twitch of his nose.

"It seemed warm and cozy up here, I suppose.

The window was open; I did not think you would mind.

It was the nearest place for shelter that I could find."

"But bats bite people's necks and get tangled in their hair!"
I said as I shivered and gave him a glare.
Sam chuckled and smiled and then said Bob Bat,
"Now, how did you ever get an idea like that?
Bats don't eat people, so let's set this right:
We only eat bugs when we fly out at night."
"What did I tell you?" asked Sam, tugging on my sleeve,
"Timmy, you have to be careful in what you believe!"

"I'm sorry," I said to Bob. "I was very wrong."
"That's okay," he replied. "We should just get along."
"Say, where did Ralph go?" suddenly asked Sam Skunk.
Then from down in my bedroom came a very loud *THUNK*.
"Oh no!" I cried out, "that sneaky raccoon slipped away!"
To Bob I called, "We are leaving, but you are welcome to stay!"

We raced down to my bedroom to find that raccoon
And saw him sitting in the window staring up at the moon.
He turned as we entered and said with an innocent face,
"I put each and every book back in its right place."
Laughing, I said, "I thought you were making trouble,
So Sam and I ran down those stairs on the double!"

"I was only trying to help," said Ralph with a bow.
"It didn't seem right to leave this mess, somehow."
"Well, thank you, my friend," I said. "That was very nice,
I'm sorry for doubting you; I should have thought twice."
Ralph Raccoon winked and waved and began to grin,
Then turned back around and left the way he came in.

I looked back at Sam, now curled up on my bed,

And gave him a friendly pat on his soft, furry head.

"Well, thank you, Timmy for letting me warm up in your bunk.

It was nice of you to share your room with a skunk."

He got up and stretched. Then, as he slowly turned,

Sam smiled and said, "Please don't forget what you've learned."

How can that be? I thought to myself,
When I saw that books had toppled from the shelf.
The books falling down must have been the noise I heard.
Then my thoughts were interrupted by one quiet word.
"Hello," said a voice, somewhat soft and meek.
From under the covers I saw two shiny eyes peek.

I was scared and about to call my brother's name,
(For whenever I did so, he usually came.)
Then I remembered he had gone to sleep away camp.
Trembling, I reached up and turned on the lamp.
There in my bunk with blankets drawn up to his nose,
Was a skunk who was shaking from his head to his toes.
"Oh my!" I cried out. "What are you doing here?"
He crept from the covers quaking with fear.

Then he scampered off and disappeared into the night.
I thought to myself that Sam was quite right.
His lesson is one I will never forget;
In fact, I shall always be in Sam's debt.

It is wrong to judge those whom you do not know
By the things people tell you that they feel are so.
Think for yourself and do not quickly judge others,
For the truth is all creatures are sisters and brothers.

— The End —